The Right Place

written by **Beatrice Masini**   illustrated by **Simona Mulazzani**

Barefoot Books
Step inside a story

When Squirrel woke up from his long rest, something didn't feel right.

His hole in the tree was still messy with dirty cups and plates everywhere, just as he'd left it before the cold came.

The outside air had the scent of melted snow and fresh green leaves. It made his hole feel dark and gloomy.

Squirrel didn't like that feeling. This hole was no longer the right place.

"Owl, where do you think the right place is?" Squirrel asked.

"ABOVE," Owl answered. "You can see and know everything from above."

Now Squirrel was very confused. How could a place be inside, above and below? Both a nest and a hole?

"Does a place like that even exist?" Squirrel asked himself.

He fell asleep thinking. As he slept in Owl's tree, above, he dreamt of a place that was both a nest and a hole, that was inside, above and below too . . .

When Squirrel
woke up, he had a plan.
He picked out a very big
tree with deep roots and
large, long branches.

"Time to get
to work," Squirrel said.
"But first, I'm going to
need some help..."

Squirrel called Woodpecker, who
drilled holes. He called Mole, who dug
tunnels. He called Bird and all her friends
to make nests. He called Turtle, who
decorated the inside. And he called Owl,
so they could have someone wise around.

When they were
all done, there were
tunnels below, nests
in the branches above
and holes inside the
big tree. Everything
was perfect.

In the big tree, everybody had a place. Everybody was happy and everybody was where they wanted to be.

"This is great," Owl said. "We can all stay together."

Squirrel finally understood what he was missing.

Before, he was alone. But now, he was with his friends.

"The right place is where we all stay together," he said.

"You said a very wise thing," Owl agreed.

And from her, that was a big compliment.

Barefoot Books
2067 Massachusetts Ave
Cambridge, MA 02140

Barefoot Books
29/30 Fitzroy Square
London, W1T 6LQ

© 2014 Carthusia Edizioni, Milano, Italy. Original title: *Il posto giusto*
Text by Beatrice Masini. Illustrations by Simona Mulazzani
Published in agreement with Phileas Fogg Agency
www.phileasfoggagency.com

Translation copyright © 2020 Barefoot Books
The moral rights of Beatrice Masini and Simona Mulazzani have been asserted

Graphic design by Elizabeth Kaleko, Barefoot Books
English-language edition edited by Nivair H. Gabriel, Barefoot Books
Translation support provided by Danielle Buonaiuto
Reproduction by Bright Arts, Hong Kong
Printed in China on 100% acid-free paper
This book was typeset in Aunt Mildred, Avenir Book, Azola La,
CCClobberin Time Crunchy, Harman Script, Pinch, Roger and Sugary Pancake
The illustrations were prepared in acrylics, pencils, pens and collage

Hardback ISBN 978-1-78285-981-9
Paperback ISBN 978-1-78285-982-6
E-book ISBN 978-1-64686-031-9

British Cataloguing-in-Publication Data: a catalogue record
for this book is available from the British Library

Library of Congress Cataloging-in-Publication Data is available under LCCN 2019044640

1 3 5 7 9 8 6 4 2

Barefoot Books
step inside a story

At Barefoot Books, we celebrate art and story that opens the hearts and minds of children from all walks of life, focusing on themes that encourage independence of spirit, enthusiasm for learning and respect for the world's diversity. The welfare of our children is dependent on the welfare of the planet, so we source paper from sustainably managed forests and constantly strive to reduce our environmental impact. Playful, beautiful and created to last a lifetime, our products combine the best of the present with the best of the past to educate our children as the caretakers of tomorrow.

www.barefootbooks.com

Beatrice Masini

is an Italian journalist, translator and
writer who has published 40 books for children
and teens in many languages. She is known for having
translated J. K. Rowling's Harry Potter series.
She lives and works in Milan, Italy.

Simona Mulazzani

has illustrated over 90 adult and children's books for
publishers around the world. In 2013 she received
a Silver Medal from the Original Art Show
at the Society of Illustrators. She lives
and works in Pesaro, Italy.